THE BEST SEL
ALMOST COOL SERIE

DIARY OF AN ALMOST COOL GIRL - 5 FUNNY BOOKS

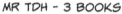

ALMOST COOL WITCH - 2 BOOKS   MR TDH - 3 BOOKS

DIARY OF AN ALMOST COOL BOY - HILARIOUS BOOKS
FOR BOTH GIRLS AND BOYS

KIDS LOVE OUR BOOKS!

Diary of an Almost Cool Girl

Book 5
New Kids in the Hood

Bill Campbell

Table of Contents

Chapter 1 - Never Accept A Dare

Kate was sitting on the table when she let out a terrifying scream. A robot shoots her with a blue light, and it hits her leg. I tried to sneak down on the other side of the table, but the robot quickly spins around to my side, and its taser tries to zap me as well. I'm too fast, and it misses me, just! Fear adds speed and agility to my normally uncoordinated body. The robot shuffles back to the door, it spins three times, and when once again facing towards us, it goes through its welcoming announcement.

"Good morning, I am Ronald. Let me help guide you through the Science Center. Which section do you wish to visit first?"

"Intruder! Intruder! Alert! Alert! I must warn you I am contacting the authorities," screeched the Robot.

It has been twenty minutes since we entered the Science Center, and Ronald The Robot ceased being a helpful guide and instead became our tormentor. At this stage, I just wish that Ronald would contact the authorities so they could save us from this crazy robot.

To be honest, I'm not unhappy that Ronald has zapped Kate many times already. She's not exactly my favorite person. However, being stuck in this Science Center is not my idea of a fun time. The robot taser hurts, and our many attempts to escape his evil clutches have so far failed and left us balanced precariously on the science table.

Many possible escape options have come to my brilliant mind, but all have involved using Kate as a decoy while I escape from Ronald, pain-free. However, Kate is not keen to sacrifice her own welfare for me, and she is such a pain, I certainly won't be doing it for her.

Ronald is on the move again, circling the table we are perched upon while blaring out, "Intruder! Intruder!"

At this stage, I'm regretting going to the Science Center after school had finished when it is strictly against our school's rules. I only did it because I didn't want Kate to get the attention of the class. Kate was the only one who had accepted Linda's dare.

"Okay, Kate, we've got to get out of here," I said. Not to mention that I was now busting to go to the toilet. A girl does have her pride. I outline my plan. It involves us both going to opposite ends of the table and, on the count of 3, jumping down and running towards the door, which is the only exit from the lab. Of course, we then have a 10-minute argument over who gets the end of the table closest to the door.

Eventually, I give in, as my need for a toilet is getting worse by the second, so carefully we wriggle to our chosen ends of the table. I slowly count to three. On three, we both hit the floor. I'm running, but Kate trips and goes sprawling onto the floor. That Ronald is a genius robot, he quickly decides to focus on me, and I never make the door. Two quick zaps on my bottom have me detouring to another table. Once I'm on the table out of reach, Ronald turns back to Kate, who has regained her feet and heading for the door.

Ronald is too fast. He heads her off with little blasts of his taser accompanied by little squeals from Kate as she runs and dives on the same table I'm already on. Great, now we are even worse off, still on a table, but even further away from the door. At least this is a bigger table, and we have room to lie down even. Hopefully, we won't have to spend the night here. There is also an empty glass beaker on the table, a pity it's not full of acid so we could dissolve old annoying Ronald.

As I wriggle around on the table, trying to contain my now frantic bladder, which desperately wants to be emptied, I notice Kate also seems to be doing her own 'I need to go' dance.

Finally, I announce, "I'm busting! I'm going to have to pee in the beaker, so look the other way".

I'll leave the rest to your imagination but squatting on a table trying to pee into a beaker while a rampaging Ronald the robot whirls around the table, and a girl you detest is sitting within arm's reach is not easy or fun. With great relief, my mission is accomplished.

Then Kate says, "Turn around. It's my turn." She finishes and asks, "We never tell anyone about this ever, agreed."

I eagerly agree. I don't want to go from 'almost cool' to 'never cool and slightly gross.'

So as we sit there with Ronald racing around endlessly, I wish my phone battery would last that long. With the smelly beaker of urine sitting between us, an idea springs into my mind. Perhaps if we throw the beaker of urine onto Ronald, as it is a watery liquid, it might cause an electric short-circuit, and Ronald might come to a smelly halt.

So starts the next argument between Kate and me. Who will throw the beaker filled with urine over Ronald? Kate doesn't want to do it in case it spills onto her hands. What, so she thinks I'm okay with urine-soaked hands? I'm not, but I've had enough of being trapped in here with her and Ronald; to be honest, I do prefer Ronald to her.

I pick up the beaker, which is surprisingly heavy, and try to aim it at Ronald. He keeps circling us, so there is no way I can guarantee to get it on him.

Reluctantly, Kate agrees to dangle down off the table to draw Ronald closer to get a better shot. I stand on the table, carefully cradling the beaker just behind Kate as she dangles her legs over to attract Ronald.

It nearly works.

Ronald races over, I take careful aim, but just as I launch our beaker of smelly destruction, Kate slips onto the floor next to Ronald. The cascade of urine falls onto Ronald, and almost immediately, there is a loud bang, with a flash of light, and then smoke starts to stream out of Ronald. His green eyes fill with what looks like urine. Yuck! He stops all sounds and movements.

Victory is ours! Humans triumph over technology!

I realize Kate is not sharing my sense of achievement as I move my vision to her sitting on the floor next to Ronald.

Collateral damage is what they call it in the movies.

Girl down!

Yes, poor old Kate has taken the same hit as Ronald, urine is still dripping off her hair, and she is making strange little ewww noises.

"Come on, Kate, let's go!" I yell, and she follows me out the door.

We pause at the main entrance to make sure no one sees us leaving the building. Kate turns to me and growls at me, "Not a word of this to anyone. It never happened, agreed?"

I nod my head, trying not to laugh, and we both head off on our separate ways home.

So I know you are wondering...who is this Kate, whom I dislike so much? Well, you need to go back to Monday when Kate first came into my life. Read on and discover why Kate is SO annoying. So annoying that I haven't even come up with a suitable nickname for her yet.

Chapter 2 - Twins Arrival

Monday

I rushed to get ready for school today, hoping that Mr. Tall Dark and Handsome, known as Mr. TDH to me, but as Richard to everyone else, would be back at school today for the new semester. I found my best friend, Gretel, waiting at the school gate for me. After a quick hug, I asked her, "Have you seen Mr. TDH yet?"

Gretel shrugged her shoulders. "Not yet, Maddi." I was disappointed but hoped he still might show up today. He had been on holiday with his parents, and I haven't seen him for weeks. I hoped that I could solve the mystery of the note he left me, which my beautiful but highly destructive puppy, Buddy, had partially chewed, destroying the last part of his message to me. The only legible part of the message was:

Dear Maddi
Thanks for always
making me laugh
and being a
great partner
in robotics.
Would you be

So, as you would understand, I'm bursting with impatience to find out what Mr. TDH was going to ask. I desperately hoped he had asked me to be his girlfriend or to be his partner at the end of the school dance or something else suitably romantic. The not knowing is driving me crazy, although my friends would probably just say crazier!

The bell rang, and we are all headed off to assembly. Gretel and I quickly found our home class and sat down. I glanced around, but there was still no sight of Mr. TDH. The teachers buzzed around the students on assembly, trying to get them to be quiet as they saw our principal, Mrs. Cook, approaching the microphone on the stage.

The nickname that I gave Mrs. Cook was Granny because that's what she looks like. Unfortunately, Mrs. Cook isn't kind and friendly, like your average grandmother.

Granny reinforced her reputation by grabbing the microphone and snarling, "Quiet!" No welcome back students and teachers. No, she launches into a tirade of how we should be all quiet when she comes to the front of the assembly.

I glanced around at the teachers, and they seemed to be as impressed by Granny's welcome as the students were. Granny spent the next 10 minutes basically reading the school rules to us. She certainly knows how to win over a crowd.

Finally, Granny said something that grabbed my attention, "We have two new students I need to introduce." She waves her hand in a come here gesture to a blonde girl and boy who were standing to the side of the assembly. They both start to walk over to her, but not quickly enough for Granny, who snaps at them, "Hurry up, I've got other things to do."

"Welcome to our school, Kate and Tate Lewis," she says, reading from a sheet of paper. "Apparently, they are twins," she announces.

She peered at them carefully and continued, "You don't look like twins to me."

The girl, Kate, leaned into the microphone and said, "We are not identical twins, but we are very similar in appearance, although I am smarter, and better looking than my brother."

Granny is obviously upset at Kate's interruption and briskly instructs us to give the new students a clap. After about three seconds, she calls out, "That will do, go to your classes!"

Gretel and I sat in the front row of our history class, listening to Mrs. Tompkins as she outlined our work units for the semester. The deputy principal, whom I nicknamed Mrs. She Who Rules the School, might have to change that nickname now that granny is our principal, walks in with the new twins, Kate and Tate.

"Great," whispered Gretel, "new potential friends." I just smile and nod. After Mrs. Tompkins had a private discussion with the twins out by her teacher's desk, she announced to the class, "Obviously, the new twins are joining your class, so I'll ask Kate and Tate to tell you a little bit about themselves, Tate, you can go first."

Before Tate can even open his mouth, Kate elbows him aside, and at machine-gun pace blurts out, "I think I should go first as I have much more to tell, and frankly, I'm much more interesting!" She continues, "At my last school, I was class captain three years in a row, I was head of the debating team, had the lead role in the school play, placed in the top five percent for Mathematics and Writing in my class, and made the finals in three athletic events at the sports carnival. And made the school swim team, and….".

14

"Well, that all sounds amazing, Kate," says Mrs. Tompkins. "We might hear from Tate now."

Tate speaks in a pleasant even voice but looks a little embarrassed to be speaking in front of a class of strangers. "Well," he says, "as you can probably guess from what Kate has told you, we came from a fairly small school."

That gets a low buzz of laughter from the class and a savage scowl from his sister Kate. "I enjoy all sports, reading, and just hanging out with my friends, which I hope you all soon will be, my friends, I mean, thanks for listening."

Mrs. Tompkins directs them to sit at the two spare desks just behind Gretel and me. I hear Kate snarl at Tate, "You sound better when you say nothing at all. I'm trying to make a good first impression."

Tate quietly and calmly replies, "You'd better keep trying then."

I notice that every time Mrs. Tompkins asks a question, Kate nearly knocks the desk over in her rush to get her hand up, and if she isn't volunteering an answer, she is asking a question. Even when Mrs. Tompkins asks for a volunteer to take a message to another class, Kate's hand is first up. Mrs. Tompkins thanks her for volunteering but says, "Since you won't know where the classroom is, you're probably not the best person to take the message."

Not to be deterred, Kate convinces Mrs. Tompkins that she should go with the other student selected to learn her way around the school. Mrs. Tompkins agrees to Kate's suggestion, but I think it was just so she could get a break from Kate. As it often seems to do on the first day back after the holidays, the time passes slowly, but eventually, history is over, and we move off to Physical Education.

Mr. Grant, our old PE teacher, has moved to another school and standing in the hall waiting for us is the new PE teacher. He is tall and looks extremely strong.

My name is Mr. Swan; he announces in a thunderous voice, his voice rivals my own Dad's. I call Dad, Mr. Boom Boom. Fortunately, an alternate nickname springs to mind, sonic, as in sonic boom. I'm such a genius at times. Mr. Sonic gives a fifteen-minute run down on his own sporting prowess ending with what we will learn is his favorite saying, "Pain is your friend."

It's okay, I figured it out, he doesn't mean real pain, like at the dentist, but the pain you get when you run and work out.

So when Mr. Sonic asks who can explain what he means by that, my hand shoots up at the speed of lightning. After all, it's always good to make a good impression on a new teacher. I explain that I agree that pain is your friend because when you feel pain, it's time to stop running or whatever activity you are doing. The loud laughter that burst from the class lets me know that my answer was obviously incorrect and unintentionally funny.

Mr. Sonic replied, "Very funny, young lady, but how about a serious answer."

Kate instantly blurts out a long-winded answer that basically meant that the pain lets you know that you were pushing your body to its limit, and that would make you stronger and fitter.

"Great answer!" booms Mr. Sonic. "Ten laps of the hall, everyone, except you." He points at Kate, "You can skip it, and tell me about your sporting achievements as you are obviously an athlete."

Mr. Sonic loves his sport and appears determined to make us all very fit as he pushes us through one exhausting activity after another. Kate has excelled in pretty much every activity, and obviously has achieved favorite status with Mr. Sonic. But he also appears to have a special interest in developing me from an uncoordinated danger girl, to someone who lives up to his pain motto. This could end up being a very long semester.

At lunch, Gretel and I sat around talking as always, I was quite surprised how much she talked about Tate. Tate's voice is really lovely. Tate was good at PE, and Tate seems very friendly.

I think Miss Gretel might have a little crush on Tate Lewis. A pity that his sister is a pain, but I don't say that to Gretel.

The twins are the center of attention at lunch and are surrounded by a bunch of students, all attempting to quiz them about pretty much everything. Watching from afar, I notice how dominant Kate is over Tate. She constantly talks over him, even when a question is directed at Tate.

The rest of the day passes quickly. I head off home, walking part of the way with Gretel. I'm keen to get home to see my puppy, Buddy, who greeted me at the door and smothered me in licks. I love dogs!

My Mom's music is blaring out, *California Dreaming*, typical of my hippie alternative Mom. I call her Mrs. Absolutely Positive because that's what she is. In her view, everything is wonderful, and everything will always turn out. Yep, I know what you are thinking. She obviously isn't living the school and social life of an 'almost cool girl,' like us.

"Maddi, your home at last! Buddy and I have missed you so much! I bet it was worthwhile because you would have had such a marvelous day, learning and socializing with your friends at school, so how wonderful was your day?"

Mom's greetings are always SO enthusiastic. Do you understand the nickname better now? I stick to the child code of conduct of replying about any parent question about school, "It was good."

After I changed my clothes, I took Buddy for a walk.

He such a beautiful dog, but he has some strange mannerisms. Every time he sees a dog coming towards us, he drops down on his tummy and waits until they reach him so that he can say hello.

Some dog owners realize what Buddy is doing, but others say, "You've walked that poor little dog too far. You should pick him up and carry him!"

I used to try and explain, but now I just nod and smile and wait until Buddy gets up again and continue our walk.

By the time I had walked home, Mom had cooked dinner. 'Cooked' is probably the wrong word. A salad turned into a power smoothie isn't really cooking. Mom is on another health fad, but I'm lucky because she has run out of kale tonight, which is my least favorite healthy food, and the smoothie isn't too bad.

Chapter 3 - Mr. TDH Is Back

Tuesday

I awoke at dawn and grabbed my prepacked bag so I would get to school nice and early.

ONLY JOKING!!!

I didn't wake up properly until the third time Mom came to my room and shook me. The second day of semester schoolitus, but eventually, I'd had my breakfast, crammed all my school supplies and lunch into my bag, and headed off to school, hoping that I would see Mr. TDH today.

My heart skipped a beat when I saw Mr. TDH standing near the school gate. He must be waiting for me, I thought, what a sweet boy. I'd finally get to ask him about what he asked me on the note.

As I got closer, I realized he was talking to someone, not just anyone, but Kate Lewis, the worse half of our new twins. GRRRRRR is what I felt, but luckily, what came out was, "Good morning Richard (slight delay) and Kate."

Richard welcomed me with a huge smile and warmly said, "Great to see you, Maddi."

Kate just said, "Yep, hi Mary, don't mean to be rude, but Richard and I are just getting to know each other, so we might talk with you later." As she said this, she grabbed Richard by the arm and dragged him away. Richard looked over his shoulder at me and shrugged his shoulders, and raised his eyebrows.

"See you soon, Maddi," he called out.

I found Gretel near the classroom, and with my mouth running at a million miles an hour, I told her what Kate had done. Tears welled in my eyes as I told her how Mr. TDH had just let Kate brush me off so rudely.

Gretel settled me down and said, "Mr. TDH was probably just overwhelmed by pushy domineering Kate. I'm sure he didn't mean to be rude."

The day got no better. Kate must have been close to developing Chronic Fatigue in her arm, as she answered every question asked in all our classes and asked more questions than everyone else combined.

In the last class of the day, Gretel leaned over and whispered into my ear, "It's lucky Kate loves the sound of her own voice because I'm pretty sure the rest of the class is over it!"

I burst out laughing, which got me a 'Shush' from the teacher and a puzzled glance from Kate. It was almost as if she knew we were talking about her. Hopefully, super hearing isn't another of her amazing skills.

Lunchtime had been equally annoying with Kate taking center stage in the eating area with a small group of girls, including Linda Douglas, and also Mr. TDH. When Gretel and I tried to join the group, Kate said aggressively, "Sorry girls, no room left here. You'll have to go and sit somewhere else."

I felt outraged, but Gretel dragged me away before I could get out a reply. We sat down by ourselves. Before I could express my anger, Tate, Kate's twin, sat down beside Gretel.

"I'm sorry, girls. I know my sister can be very bossy and even a little rude at times, but she can have a big heart, sometimes," said Tate with a kind smile. I stopped myself from telling him he must be delusional to think Kate has any type of heart, because he is obviously very nice and caring, and it wouldn't be fair to blame him for his sister's actions.

Anyway, although my lunchtime was ruined, Gretel had a wonderful time chatting with Tate.

Meanwhile, I'm close enough to hear Kate's loud voice as she entertains Mr. TDH and the people in that group with amazing stories about how wonderful she is. Going back into the classroom is almost a relief.

Finally, the school day ends, and I race out the gate as fast as I can. I hear Mr. TDH call my name as I cross the road, but I pretend not to hear him and keep going.

Wednesday

I left for school without the enthusiasm I had yesterday. I arrived just as the bell goes. When I take my seat next to Gretel, most of the class are already at their desks. Kate obviously had a brain-healthy breakfast because, in the first thirty minutes, she answered five questions from the teacher, asked six questions of her own, and volunteered to do two messages for the teacher. So basically, Kate is a class of one, which in some ways takes a lot of pressure off for the rest of the students to respond to Mrs. Tompkins.

Lunch was an interesting study of Kate's dynamics. When she tried to gather a group together, most of them shied away from her and sat elsewhere, including Mr. TDH. Eventually, she gathered a few together, including Linda Douglas, but thankfully Mr. TDH chose to come and sit with us. I generously decided to forgive Mr. TDH for ditching us yesterday, and soon Gretel, Mr. TDH, and I had settled back into our regular friendly conversations.

I kept trying to give Gretel hints to provide me with a moment alone with Mr. TDH, so I could try and bring up the mysterious message issue. I tried, "Gretel, do you need to go to the toilet?" She looked at me strangely, obviously wondering about my sudden interest in her toilet functions but declined to go.

Then I tried, "Gretel, did you read that poster on the wall over there? It's about the importance of washing your hands properly to prevent spreading the flu. It's really interesting."

That won me another confused look before she replied in a slightly insulted tone, "I always wash my hands!"

Luckily before I could further irritate my best friend, Kate and her small group came across and crowded around us. "There you are, Richard. I wondered where you were hiding. Linda has just dared me to sneak into the new School Science Centre after school. Get in, have a quick look around, maybe move some furniture around to play with the teachers' heads, and get a couple of selfies as proof we went in. So, Richard, how brave are you? No one else is game."

Mr. TDH replied in a nervous voice, "No way, Mrs. Cook loves that center! I'm not going in there. She would probably give you detention until you're twenty-one."

Suddenly, another voice blurts out, "I'll go with you!" My brain catches up slowly. That was my voice! What have I done?

About the same time, Gretel's foot slams into my leg as she hisses to me, "Don't be a fool."

Too late! That's me, the fool, can't back out in front of Mr. TDH and let Kate look braver than me. So before you know it, Kate and I are planning how to begin my life of crime, breaking into the Science Center.

Now the Science Center is almost brand new. Mrs. Cook received some kind of special grant from some computer company, so it has the latest and best computers, microscopes, and even a talking robot that doubles as a guide and security guard.

Kate seems to have done this type of thing before and explains we must unlock one of the side exit doors during school time so we can get in after school. "So Maddi," Kate announces in front of everyone, "you get the door unlocked, and I'll meet you in the trees beside the building twenty minutes after school finishes."

Of course, like a brain-dead zombie, what could I say, except, "Sure, easy."

The bell rings to end lunch, fortunately, before I can commit to any other foolhardy arrangements. All the way back to class, Gretel is insisting I pull out of the *Great Science Center Break-in*, but I couldn't. I know that's stupid, but I'm just sick of Kate being the center of everything.

After a while, I ask to go to the bathroom, but I race off to the Science Center. I pull a sheet of paper out of my pocket and fold it in half. The paper is my excuse for wandering around the building. If questioned, I will say I'm taking a note to the janitor from my teacher, and as the janitor could be anywhere on the school grounds, it was the perfect alibi.

Then I stumble across a teacher who has Ronald the Robot in pieces on a table. Luckily, it's Mrs. Smith, one of the nice ones. Not all teachers are mean, just most. I am only joking, trying to fit into my bad girl image. I actually really like most of my teachers. Anyway, Mrs. Smith asks what I'm doing wandering around. I nervously tell her the story about the janitor note, hoping she won't ask to see it.

"Oh, what a pity, you just missed the janitor. He just left a minute ago, and he was helping me with this robot."

I let out a sigh. That was a close call. I would have been caught out badly with my note excuse. "Never mind," continues Mrs. Smith. "While you are here, hold this motherboard in place while I screw Ronald back together."

"What's wrong with him?" I asked. Mrs. Smith explained that the robot keeps malfunctioning and doing all sorts of weird things. "Because he is the most impressive part of the Science Centre, in the eyes of Mrs. Cook, I need to fix him. Otherwise, he is a very expensive doorstop."

Great, I thought, if Ronald The Robot isn't working, it might make it easier for Kate and me.

As I helped Mrs. Smith, I looked around the room and realized that the exit door was just behind where I stood with a tinge of excitement. While Mrs. Smith used the cordless drill, I reached over and unlocked the door. The racket of the drill drowned out the door lock making a clicking noise.

I was impressed with myself.

Maddi Bull – Master Criminal!

A few minutes later, Mrs. Smith no longer needs my help and sends me on my way. I race back to class. Obviously, I have been a lot longer than the average toilet break, so the teacher asks if I'm okay. I told him my stomach was a bit off. As I walk past Kate, I give her the thumbs up. Secret agent Maddi is on fire.

After school, Gretel was still trying to talk me out of entering the Science Centre, but against all sense and personal desire to do the right thing, I insist I had to do it. Even Gretel's goodbye was another attempt to deter me, as she called, "Don't worry, I'll visit you in jail."

I waved and headed to wait in the small group of trees near the Science Centre exit door that I had unlocked.

I had started to think that Kate had decided not to come when she suddenly appeared beside me. I jumped up and let out a little scream.

"Shush," she snarled at me.

Good to see that our shared adventure wasn't going to change our relationship. At least I could see that Kate was also nervous, when in a quaking voice, she asked, "Is it all clear?"

"Yes," I responded. "Let's go!" Suddenly eager to get it over and done with. We quickly darted to the door. I kind of hoped it had been relocked, but when I turned the handle, the door opened smoothly. We snuck inside and were relieved to discover the room was empty. Even Ronald The Robot wasn't on the table anymore. We then headed down the hallway when suddenly I heard a noise coming our way, just around the corner. "Quick this way," I whispered to Kate and led her through the doorway into a larger classroom with lots of big worktables.

I could still hear the noise approaching, so I told Kate to shut the door. She grabbed the door and started to swing it shut when Ronald The Robot sped through the closing door. The door swung shut with a solid clunk. Kate ran to jump on a table as Ronald fired off his taser.

Anyway, you know the rest, our unpleasant smelly escape by knocking out Ronald with a urine bomb, and our mutual agreement never to tell anyone. Of course, the next day at school was never going to be good.

Chapter 4 - Investigation

Thursday

As I arrived at school, I couldn't help but notice the police tape across the Science Center entrance and across the side exit door that Kate and I had used yesterday.

Shortly after our classes began in the morning, an announcement came over the PA system. In an angry tone, Mrs. Cook announced, "All classes are to report to the assembly area immediately!" Even the teachers showed signs of stress as they escorted their students to assembly. Everyone realized from the PA message that Mrs. Cook was not happy. That was a worry because the closest Mrs. Cook ever got to happiness was most other people's horrible mood.

As the classes moved into their places, Mrs. Cook paced up and down out the front of the assembly area. One of her hands held the microphone while the other was clenched into a tight fist.

When all were seated, she started to talk, "Yesterday some people broke into our new Science Centre and destroyed Ronald the Robot! The police have asked me not to give out details, but as no locks were damaged, it is a high possibility that this was an inside job. Any student involved in this incident, or even has knowledge that this incident was planned, will be expelled from my school! Does anyone want to own up and confess now? Or do you want to wait until the police investigation discovers who you are?"

A silence fell over the entire assembly. Mrs. Cook let it hang for about a minute, then barked out, "The guilty will be found out, dismissed!"

As we moved back to class, Kate appeared next to me and whispered, "Say nothing. They can't prove anything."

I just nodded. My parents won't be happy if they find out what I did, and if I get expelled, it will be even worse. I worried that people would notice Kate whispering to me, but as I looked around, nearly everyone was whispering to someone.

The break-in was the biggest news we have had at our school for a long time. I felt sure that Kate wouldn't confess, but I wondered if anyone else would tell Mrs. Cook that Kate and I did it. But then I realized because Mrs. Cook had warned that anyone who knew it was planned would also be punished, that no one would tell, or they would get the same punishment.

Lunchtime was a very quiet affair, with everyone being careful not to talk about the break-in. Even Kate dropped her dominant voice level. The rest of the day passed quickly. When I returned home, I said a mumbled "Hi," to Mom, grabbed Buddy, and headed off for a long walk. When I returned home, I diverted my Mom's conversation to telling her all about my walk with Buddy, so the topic of my day at school didn't come up.

Friday

The previous two days at school had been very stressful!

Granny had been on the warpath, giving out time-outs like lollies at a birthday party. Seriously, one kid was given lunchtime detention because she had a smudge on her eyeglasses, while another boy got one because his shoelaces weren't tied up well enough.

So, when our morning class was interrupted by an announcement for a whole school assembly, we all felt very nervous. As our room was closest to the assembly area, our class ended sitting right up the front.

Granny stood at the front with a triumphant-looking smirk on her face. Just behind her was a table with lots of small plastic jars, and next to the table were a man and a lady in white overalls.

I stared at the lady, trying to read the writing on her folder, but couldn't make it out. So, I asked Gretel if she was able to read it.

Gretel squinted at the lady for a while and slowly read out the writing, Amco Laboratories Forensic, and DNA testing.

My brain went into panic mode! Obviously, Kate and I would have left our DNA all over Ronald the Robot. A glance at Kate showed that she also realized we were about to be discovered. There was nothing we could do about it. Granny had earlier in the year banned students from leaving the assembly for toilet or drink breaks.

Granny then started to speak through the microphone, "Attention students, as you all know, we have been trying to discover the criminals who destroyed Ronald in the Science Center. These experts from Amco Laboratories have discovered traces of DNA on the remains of Ronald. So, in order to eliminate you, my students, we want to compare your DNA to the DNA traces discovered.

I'm done, no escape! I'll be expelled from school and grounded forever by my parents.

Suddenly, I'm saved by an unlikely hero, the Deputy Principal, Mrs. She Who Rules the School (so nicknamed because, with our previous principal, she ran the school while he high-fived the students), almost sprints over to Granny. Granny, who was never good with technology, leaves the microphone on, so we can hear their entire conversation.

Mrs. She Who Runs the School asks, "What on Earth are you doing? It's illegal to take DNA from children without their parents' consent!"

Granny replies, "But, I'm their principal, and I'm sure some of them are involved!"

"Great!" yells the deputy. "Take their DNA, but I'm pretty sure the law will see that as a more serious crime than weeing on a robot, who didn't even work properly anyway!"

The whole assembly sat in silent astonishment, listening to the conversation between our school leaders. In fact, that's the quietest they've been all year. Granny suddenly looked up and gazed out at the sea of faces staring at her. Finally, she realized that the mike was still on. She snarls, "Assembly dismissed!" And she storms off to her office.

That was the last official mention of the notorious Science Centre break-in. Occasionally the kids spoke about it, but eventually, even that died away, much to my relief.

Chapter 5 - Maddi Bull Extreme Athlete

Monday

There was a steady stream of parents waiting outside Granny's office this morning. Apparently, parents didn't like the idea of their children's DNA being collected. The rumor mill was in overdrive!

Granny was going to be fired as principal.

Granny was going to jail.

The parents were going to sue Granny and the school.

The end result wasn't as dramatic but still a good outcome for us, the students. It was announced over the PA system that all future assemblies would be run by our deputy principal. That announcement was enough to bring a smile to most students' faces, but we were wise enough not to cheer. I even noticed our teacher react with sly grins.

Lunchtime was much improved. Kate was a lot quieter, and Mr. TDH sat with Gretel, Tate, and me. We had a lovely time, but there was no opportunity to ask Mr. TDH about the message that Buddy had destroyed. To be honest, I'm a little puzzled as to why he hasn't brought it up in conversation himself.

Kate is still painful in the classroom. Getting to answer or ask a question, or to volunteer for a job, is like a competition for her. I assume you all know someone like that. At first, you think: fine, I can relax knowing I don't have to answer anything or even ask a question because you know that within their 101 questions, sooner or later, your question will be covered.

The message jobs are, however, highly desirable, a chance to aimlessly wander around the school, taking the longest possible route to get to where you have to go, escaping the claustrophobic classroom, and being free. So you would understand that her classroom dominance was beginning to get under my skin.

In every class, no matter how fast I reacted or how hard I tried, Kate beat me to the question or the message job every time. I was feeling so over her! She made me feel sick! I felt like yelling at her to go away, forever!

When I got home, I googled tips for getting your hand up first...but found nothing. So I did arm exercises and practiced putting up my arm as fast as I could.

Tuesday

Mr. Swan had organized for a junior ninja course to visit the school. They had arrived at school early and erected it on the school oval. It looked amazing, just like the ninja courses you see on TV, just slightly downsized. The whole school has assembled on the raised grassy banks overlooking the oval.

Mr. Swan introduced the man in charge. "Give a big welcome to Mr. Lee," he announced.

"Thanks, Mr. Swan, but please, everyone just calls me Jagger," he replied. Jagger had a tall and very athletic body. He also had a winning toothpaste advertisement smile.

Jagger clipped on a portable microphone and continued, "Mr. Swan asked me to explain the course, but the first thing you must know is that unlike the Television version, if you fall or fail an obstacle, you're not eliminated. You are allowed three more tries, and after that, if you still haven't been able to master it, you can walk around it and continue on with the course. As I said, Mr. Swan asked me to explain the course, but the best way to do that is for me to explain while a volunteer does the course. So who wants to volunteer?"

Yesterday's practice with raising my arm paid off. My arm shot up like a rocket from NASA. Along with a million other hands, but Jagger pointed at me and called me over. "What's your name?" he asked. My mind was racing, my thoughts a blur. I did it. I out-volunteered Kate, and in fact, most of the school. Then another thought, what had I done? I'd volunteered to do a ninja course! In front of the whole school, where my lack of sporting ability is almost legendary- the only gold medal I'm likely to win is one for being uncoordinated.

As I consider the awful situation I've put myself in, Jagger repeated his question, "What's your name?"

This time I register that Jagger is talking to me, and I managed to get out a mumbled, "Maddi."

"Great name, now let's go and get onto this course," he booms. The watching students let out an excited cheer, and I feel the pressure build.

So Jagger's plan was for me to do the course while he did a running commentary. This was looking like a potential ten out of ten on the die of embarrassment scale. "Ok, everyone, the first thing all of you have to do is a warm-up and stretch." He then leads me through a little jog around the course and a series of arm and leg stretches.

After that, my body was ready to lie down and have a rest, but instead, Jagger moved me on to the first obstacle of the course. A series of balance beams linked together over some soft mats in case you fall (or, in my case - when you fall). The beams got narrower as you go along, so I was almost at the end when I fell.

This pleased Jagger greatly because he got to remind everyone that they had to start again if that happened to them. "Remember, you have three goes, and if you still can't do it, you have to skip the obstacle."

I managed to reach the end on my second go and moved on to a climbing wall by some luck. I made it over the wall on my third attempt, but my energy was fading fast.

The next obstacle was a rope swing over a pit of what looked like green slime, "Don't worry," announced Jagger, "it washes out easily."

I had to run and grab the rope, which was partly over the pit. The momentum from the run should be enough to enable you to swing to the other side of the slime pit.

Unfortunately, the momentum from my first try wasn't enough. I ended up dangling motionless over the pit, no way out except down. So, I let go of the rope and fell into the slime pit. When I emerged, covered in bright green slime, everyone burst into laughter.

My second attempt was better, except I let go of the rope too soon and fell back into the pit that caused an "OOOOH" from the watching crowd.

Jagger happily announced, "The slime washes out of your hair easily too."

The third attempt saw me make the other side despite my slime-covered clothes and hair. I made it through the rest of the obstacles with not too much difficulty or further embarrassment, with Jagger's running commentary. I approached the final obstacles with a heaving chest and shaking arms and legs.

The last obstacle was a ramp that started steep but ended almost like a vertical wall with a rope ladder hanging from just below the top. Apparently, all I had to do was accelerate to the speed of an Olympic sprinter up the ramp, make a leap like a gymnast, grab the rope ladder, and climb up and over.

"Simple," said Jagger.

My first two attempts were terrible failures. I didn't get anywhere near the end of the rope ladder. It was then that Jagger announced, "This is the most difficult obstacle of the entire course. Only five percent of people who attempt it are successful."

Quietly just to me, Jagger said, "You can skip your last go if you wish. I'll just say we need to get everyone else started."

There was my way out. I could be one of the majority, one of the ninety-five percent who fails. I thought of Kate, who had annoyed me so much that I had volunteered to be the crash test dummy for the course. And I thought of all the times the 'almost cool girls' like me and you, get overlooked and laughed at.

I shook my head at Jagger. I wanted my final attempt. He smiled at me and quietly said, "Pump with your arms as you run and aim for the middle of the ramp, and don't leap until you start to feel your speed dropping off. And most importantly, believe in yourself."

I followed Jagger's instructions and gave it everything I had. As I felt my hands connect with the rope, I screamed out in victory. I carefully held on as I climbed up the rope ladder and the over on to the top of the wall. I raised both arms in elation and heard the cheers of the rest of the school.

Jagger gave me a high-five as I walked back to the assembled students. Gretel ran up and hugged me. "You were amazing!" she squealed.

Mr. TDH was beside Gretel. He smiled and patted me on the shoulder. "You never cease to amaze me!"

Kate walked past me with a strange look on her face. "Well, I must admit you certainly surprised me. I didn't think you had it in you," she said, looking back at me.

What a great day, we all thought Mr. Swan was the best teacher in the entire world for organizing Jagger and his ninja course to visit our school. Everyone enjoyed it. There was a great atmosphere as Mr. Swan thanked Jagger on the students' behalf, we all gave him a huge cheer. Everyone getting through the course took half the school day, and Mr. Swan and the teachers sent us off to lunch.

My moment of fame had faded away, but I still felt the buzz of being successful at something that I thought I couldn't do. Maybe my Mom was right. To succeed at anything, all you have to do is not give up and keep going even if you fail at first.

At lunch, I was sitting with Gretel and Mr. TDH when Gretel stood up and announced she was going to the toilet and would be back soon. At last, alone with Mr. TDH. I would be able to ask about the message and what it said on the part that Buddy had devoured.

"So Richard," (naturally, I don't call him MR. TDH to his face, that would be way too embarrassing and awkward) I nervously started. "I never got a chance to thank you for the lovely card you gave me at the costume ball dance."

His face went bright red straight away, and he looked away from me. Then he said, "I'm glad you liked it."

Oh no, I thought; he is embarrassed about the message and probably regretted giving it to me. But I still desperately wanted to know what he had written on the card. So I kept going. "You know how Buddy likes to chew up everything in reach. Well, when I got home, I had to do the dishes, and I left your card in my bedroom. While I was gone, Buddy jumped up on my bed and chewed up the card. I managed to rescue most of it, but the bottom part ended up in Buddy's stomach. I wasn't able to read the whole of your message or the question you asked."

"That Buddy! Remember when he peed on my shirt, and then he destroyed my card. I'm beginning to think he's got something against me." He laughed.

"So, what did you..." I began to ask, when not only did Gretel return, but so did Kate, Tate, and two other girls.

There goes any privacy I had, and I didn't finish my question. Tate took over the conversation by asking Mr. TDH, "What was your favorite part of the course?"

Shortly after, the bell rang, and we headed back to class. And I still don't know what Mr. TDH was asking me in his message.

After school, we all headed our separate ways home, so there was no further chance to talk to Mr. TDH.

At home, I made the mistake of telling Mom how well I did on the ninja course. She started googling to see if there were any ninja clubs or training groups I could join. I had to slow her down before she had mapped out a new future for me as a professional ninja warrior.

Chapter 6 - Overseas Students

Monday

Sorry Diary, I haven't had time to write over the past few days, Mom has been on a clean-up-the-house mission, and so between school and house duties, all of my free time had vanished.

Mom's usually reasonably relaxed about tidiness. It's her inner hippie thing she has going, but she becomes an entirely different person if anyone is scheduled to visit.

So, it was no real surprise when Dad calmly mentioned that his old friend from university might drop in on Sunday, that I saw the transformation into super cleaning woman occur, right before my eyes.

In the middle of breakfast on Wednesday morning, Mom, on hearing Dad's news got up and started dusting and vacuuming while we were all still eating.

I was reminded to be home straight after school, as I would have to clean my room.

Dad gulped his breakfast down fast, obviously keen to escape before he was swept up in the cleaning roster.

Saturday

The previous afternoon's and evening's cleaning paled into insignificance with the Saturday morning perfect storm of cleaning.

Dad and I were assigned set tasks, and when Dad suggested the house was probably clean enough, Mom's out-of-character explosion convinced Dad to keep cleaning.

Buddy and Tyson were exiled to the yard, and neither were happy with that decision.

By the afternoon, the entire house was sparkling clean, floors mopped, everything dusted, windows washed, and Dad and I collapsed onto the couch.

Mom finished her final inspection, looked at us lying on the couch, and ordered, "Up you two, that yard is a mess! Get out there and clean it up."

We slowly dragged our weary bodies outside. While Dad got out the lawnmower, I picked up palm branches and raked up leaves on the lawn.

Finally, we had finished, I escaped any further work by taking the dogs for a walk while Dad hid in the shed pretending to work on the mower.

Sunday

At 10 am, Dad's friend called to say that he wouldn't make it around as he had to go to work as his workmate was sick. AHHHHH, all that work for nothing!

When I grow up, I'll just keep one room perfectly tidy in my house and will only use it if a visitor comes. That way, housework will be minimal, and I won't have to use my children as slaves.

Mom and Dad laughed when I told them my future plan, but they often don't see the greatness in my ideas.

Monday

On assembly this morning, the Deputy, She Who Rules the School, made an exciting announcement. "Arrangements had been made for our school to host some students from Japan. The Japanese students have learned English as a second language at their school so that communication will be easy. The idea is that each visiting student will live with a family from our school while they are visiting for two weeks. If this program is successful, then perhaps in the future, some of our students may be able to do a return exchange in Japan."

A buzz of excitement ran through the assembled students as we considered the possibilities. The deputy also informed us that the school digital newsletter sent out this morning contained further information on the Japanese student visit and an application form to be a host family.

All day, the only focus of student conversation was about the Japanese students. Everyone hoped they would get to have a student stay with them. Kate announced that her family should get to host two students since she was a twin, and she shouldn't have to share just one Japanese student with her brother, Tate.

That brought a groan from everyone listening, including her brother Tate, who replied, "Come on, Kate, you're just plain embarrassing now."

As soon as the day was over, I raced home with the plan of asking Mom if we could apply to host one of the visitors. I burst into the house and blurted out, "Mom, can we let one stay with us?"

Mom was unusually vague, "I don't know what you are talking about, Maddi," she replied.

"It's in the newsletter!" I desperately continued. Mom gave me the 'mom lecture' on how busy she had been all day, and perhaps if I did more to help around the house, she would have more time to turn on her computer and read the newsletter.

So naturally, I said, "I'll help now. What would you like me to do?"

Mom quickly listed off a mountain of jobs I could do and set me to work.

Dad came home, and I heard them talking in hushed tones in the kitchen as I folded up the washing in the laundry. By the time I had finished all the jobs, it was dinner time. As we sat down to eat, I tried to ask again about the Japanese students, but Dad interrupted and started talking about how nice dinner was. Every time I tried to speak, either Mom or Dad would interrupt again. They were driving me mad! I tried one more time, but Dad butted in again. Then both of them burst out laughing.

What is going on, I thought?

Mom said, "Enough teasing, just tell her before she has a meltdown."

Dad smiled. "Okay, Madonna just relax, your mom has already filled in the application to host an exchange student, she rang me at work, and we agreed it would be a wonderful experience."

I let out a squeal of excitement and hugged them both. I even forgave them for teasing me. Now you know where I get my weird sense of humor.

Thursday

All week everyone at school had been focused on one topic, the exchange student program.

Nearly everyone I had spoken to said that their family had put in an application to host a Japanese student, which made me wonder if there would be more host families than Japanese students.

Today, my worst fears became a reality when Mrs. She Who Rules the School put out an announcement over the PA system. She announced to the school, "I'm very proud of our school community as fifty-five families offered to host a visiting Japanese student. Unfortunately, only thirty Japanese students will visit our school, so obviously, some families who volunteered will not be able to host a student. Mrs. Cook and I decided the best and fairest way to decide which families would be allocated a student was to do it by ballot. That means that we will put all the names of the families who offered to host a student in a container and then randomly select the names of thirty families from the container. To make sure this is fair, the ballot will be conducted on assembly on Monday."

The announcement created a storm of conversations that spread around the room before Miss Butcher instructed us to quieten down and get on with our work.

Monday

The students gathered on assembly fell into silence as Mrs. Cook and Mrs. She Who Rules the School arrived with a plastic container. Mrs. Cook gave a rambling speech about the democratic process and how lucky the school was to have some of its families get the opportunity to interact with the visiting students. Mrs. She Who Rules the School tries to soften the blow by announcing that the families who miss out this time will be first on the list next time.

Mrs. Cook spoils it by butting in with, "If the exchange happens again next year."

Mrs. Cook started to pull names from the container and handed them to her deputy, who announces the names to the assembly. Of course, Kate's family's name is the first name called out.

Now that she no longer has any further interest in who else gets called out, she starts talking in a loud voice about all the plans she has to amaze and entertain the lucky student who gets her family. Several others tried to shush her, as we struggle to hear the names called because of her chatter.

My stress levels build as we reached number 24, and my name still hadn't been pulled out. Number 26 was Mr. TDH, and although I felt happy for him, I secretly wished it had been me.

I missed the names number 27 and 28 because Kate called out to Mr. TDH, "We'll have to get together and do some stuff with our students."

But the squeals of excitement from other classes let me know my name hadn't been called. Number 29 went to another class as well, so one last chance remained.

Gretel and I held hands as Mrs. She Who Rules the School took the last name handed to her by Mrs. Cook. "The final family to host a student will be," a slight pause, "Madonna Bull's family." I breathed a huge sigh of relief.

I saw tears forming in Gretel's eyes, so I whispered to her, don't worry, you almost live at our place. We'll both get to spend a lot of time with the student.

That afternoon, the students whose families had been picked had to attend a meeting with the deputy, where we were given a mountain of paperwork for our parents to fill out. She told us that the students would be arriving at our school next Monday afternoon. Our parents would have to pick up the students and their luggage and transport them to our homes. As well we were told there would be some organized functions for the Japanese students and their host families.

Mom was nearly as excited as me when I arrived home and told her the good news. Her excitement slightly diminished when I showed her the paperwork. But then Mrs. Absolutely Positive kicked in, and she said, "Nothing good comes without some effort, so it is all good."

Dad was pretty excited too when he heard the news, as were the dogs Tyson and Buddy, even if they didn't have a clue why we were excited, but they just picked up the good vibes.

Mrs. Absolutely Positive quickly transformed into Mrs. Practical/ Drill Sergeant and soon had my Dad and me clearing out the spare room. We shifted in a cupboard and made up the bed in there (that was normally a dumping ground for anything that didn't have a proper home). Mom then took over and did the finer finishing touches, folding the sheets down, folding the bath towel into a swan shape, and arranging the pillows into an artistic formation to please the fussiest designer.

Finally, declaring the room was actually fit for human habitation.

Chapter 7 - Konnichiwa

Monday

After what seemed so many long days of waiting, finally, the arrival of the Japanese students was imminent. We all have been so excited, and even I made it to school early. The Japanese students were meant to arrive during the morning and rather than appear at an assembly. They would be given a tour around the classes and introduced to the students. At lunchtime, those students who were lucky enough to be picked out to host a Japanese student would get to eat a special lunch with their buddy student.

The Japanese students were brought to the classes in two groups, fifteen in each group, along with a Japanese teacher for each group. The first group arrived at our class at about ten o'clock, they appeared nervous and were very polite as they introduced themselves. We were invited to ask questions, and it quickly became apparent from these attempts at communication that some of our visitors weren't as good at English as we expected.

I stared at the students, wondering if my host student was in this group or the other group. Not knowing was frustrating, but I had to just wait until lunchtime to meet my new Japanese friend. The second group was just as lovely as the first, with a similar level of language skills. It occurred to me that living with someone when you had trouble understanding each other might be difficult.

Lunch was set up in the school hall with several long tables, tablecloths, and close by another table without chairs but filled with an array of food. When we arrived at the hall, we were met by the deputy, Mrs. She Who Runs the School. She explained that the Japanese students were already sitting at the tables, and we would find a place marker with our name on it, the student to the left of our place marker would be the student we were to host. Their name would also be on the place marker, underneath our own. She reminded us to use our best manners, introduce ourselves, and to talk to our visitors as much as possible. It would be our job to guide our students to the food and help them with their lunch selections.

The deputy then told us to find our places and sit down. That was followed by, "Walk, don't run!"

We raced off to find our names. I found my name towards the end of the first table, seated to my left, was a girl with long shiny dark pulled into two pigtails. As I sat down, she gave me a nervous smile and a slight head bow. I glanced back at the place marker and saw that her name was Kamiko. I said, "Hi, my name is Maddi, it's lovely to meet you, Kamiko."

When she replied, I let out a sigh of relief. Her English was quite good, with a cute little accent and a soft, pleasant voice. "I'm so glad to meet you, Maddi. It is a great honor to visit your school."

As instructed, I took Kamiko over to the food area and tried to help her pick out some lunch.

The food table was loaded up with yummy food, fried chicken, hamburgers, spaghetti, wraps, salads, fish, and even sushi. I tried to describe all the different meal options, but Kamiko still looked confused.

She must have been hungry because she picked out a piece of pizza, fried chicken, cheese dip, and a tuna salad. I just grabbed a hamburger, and we moved back to our seats.

Kamiko bit into the pizza first and started spluttering straight away. She grabbed her glass of water and emptied it in one gulp. "Hot!" she exclaimed.

Next, she tried the fried chicken, which she declared, "Yummy," with a big smile. She ate the tuna salad next and commented that the tuna tasted funny. "Oh, that's right, you Americans cook your tuna. That is why it tastes different. In our sushi, the tuna is not cooked only marinated."

Kamiko took a tentative bite of a corn chip covered with cheese dip, and she obviously liked it, as she quickly demolished the rest very quickly. "Your food is so tasty and varied," she gushed enthusiastically.

So lunch ended on a positive note, and when Mrs. She Who Rules the School thought we had all finished eating, she announced that we were now to take our Japanese students back to our classroom where they would stay until school ended.

Excitedly we walked our visitors to the classrooms. Our teacher, who had several visiting students in her class, gave up teaching her planned lesson. Instead, she got each host to introduce their visiting student to the class, and then we played some simple get-to-know-you games.

The time went quickly, and after the bell rang, Kamiko and I went to the staff room where the Japanese students had left their suitcases. Once Kaminko had collected her luggage, we made our way out to the gate for Mom to pick us up.

Mom arrived and burst out of the car in a cloud of noise, "Oh, oh, oh! Maddi, she is so beautiful. I can't wait to take her home and show the neighbors."

"Mom!" I whispered through my teeth. "She is a person, not something to put on display!"

Kaminko just stood there blushing.

Mom managed to overcome her natural enthusiasm and introduced herself to Kaminko, who bowed politely as she introduced herself to Mom.

Mom went back into *normal mode* for the car trip home and managed to restrict herself to fifty questions to Kaminko. Kaminko smiled all the way home and seemed relaxed, so perhaps Moms all around the world are the same.

Kaminko was very impressed with her bedroom.

She loved our pet dog Buddy but seemed a little scared of our other dog Tyson, the giant black Great Dane. She said she had never seen a dog so tall and that her family didn't have any pets.

Luckily, when Dad came home, he wasn't as overwhelmed as Mom by our visitor and treated her like any of my other friends.

After dinner, Kaminko and I sat in my room and chatted.

She said I had a very nice family and a lovely house and that I was lucky to have two pet dogs. She said she was an only child and lived in an apartment.

"I have never had a pet," she said sadly.

It made me think how lucky I was to live here, surrounded by my family and pets, with all the love they gave me.

Chapter 8 - Mom Friendship Disaster

Each day we went with our exchange students to school, they would spend some time in the class of their host student, and for the rest of the school day, as a group working on their English skills and learning about American culture.

Everything was going along fine. The visitors were happy and having a great time, the hosts were happy and enjoying their interactions with the Japanese students.

The only slight annoyance was Kate. She constantly told all of us how her student was the best, the smartest, the funniest, and that her student was, of course, having a much better time with Kate than any of the other Japanese students were having with their hosts.

Then one day after school…disaster struck.

I arrived home with Kaminko to see a sleek Mercedes Benz sports car parked out the front of our house. Mom was entertaining a guest. As we entered, I heard a loud female voice saying, "Well, it's been wonderful meeting you. I have to get going, I've got my cross-fit training class on soon, so I'll see you on Saturday."

A tall fit-looking blonde woman rushed past me in the hallway, "Hi Maddy, catch you on Saturday."

As she went out our front door, I asked Mom who that was. "Well, Maddi, that was the mother of your friends, Kate and Tate, and you are going to be so excited because she has organized a party for all the visiting students and their host families at her house on Saturday."

Great, thanks to Mom, I would get to spend time with Kate out of school. Yay!

Mom continued, "She seemed a lovely person. I can see us being good friends."

Fantastic, I thought, perhaps I can go and live in Japan with Kamiko.

Saturday

As Dad drove us closer to Kate's house, the neighborhood got more and more prestigious. Finally, we arrived at Kate's address: 23 Sycamore Row, to discover that Kate lived in a mansion three stories high and surrounded by manicured green lawns and lush gardens.

Dad drove slowly up the long-curved driveway and parked in the parking area opposite the front entrance. Yes, they actually had a parking area with white lines and all.

No butler appeared at the door to greet us, but perhaps it was his day off, so Dad pressed the doorbell, and shortly after, Tate opened the door. "Hi, Maddi and Kamiko, and Mr. and Mrs. Bull. Please follow me around to the back garden. That's where we are having the party," he announced very formally.

We followed around the side of the house to find a massive pool area, surrounded by colored marques, under which already sat many of the invited families and students.

"Please make yourself at home, and you'll find food and drinks on the tables," Tate informed us. Mom and Dad headed over to talk with some parents they knew, and Kamiko and I headed over to where most of the kids had gathered, near the other side of the pool.

Kate was standing in front of a semi-circle of students. Most of them looking as awestruck as I felt. Their house and gardens were incredible. I felt like we were on the set of a Hollywood movie. We arrived just in time to hear Kate say, "Of course, our old house was much bigger than this little place, but this was the best we could get on short notice, so I guess we'll just have to slum it for now."

Kate then led us to a games area where they had set up games of quoits, bocce, and a giant game of twister that 16 people could play at once. Kate, of course, excelled at all the games, and the most common thing heard was Kate announcing, 'I won again!' When I was playing twister, Kate managed a sneaky shoulder barge that sent me tumbling to the mat. "You're out!" screeched Kate with a sly smile on her face.

Finally, her competitive urges satisfied, Kate introduced a new game, the mummy. She organized us all into groups and gave each group a pile of toilet paper rolls. I was surprised when she put me in her group with Mr. TDH. Perhaps I should have guessed then that this game would not turn out well for me.

Kate quickly explained the game. "Each team has ten minutes to wrap up one person in toilet paper to look like an Egyptian Mummy, and about then, I grew suspicious of why she chose me to be in her group. She told the teams they each had to select the person in their group to be the mummy, and we would start in one minute.

So Kate then says, "Maddi, you can be our Mummy."

I start to protest, "I would prefer not to, as I'm a bit claustrophobic."

"Okay, Maddi, if you're too scared of a bit of toilet paper, I guess we'll have to choose someone else, Katie announces.

"No, I'll do it! I'm not scared," I reply. Moments later, as the group starts to wrap the toilet paper around my legs, and

Kate directs them with a sinister smile, I curse myself for saying I'd do it.

Quickly my group, with much laughter at my expense, has my body almost completely covered by toilet paper. The only part not covered is the narrow band where my eyes are.

My arms are held stiffly out the front by the tightly wrapped toilet paper. I know now why Kate put me in her group. I'm certainly not looking my elegant best.

Tate announces, "Everyone, time is up. Help them stand up so we can all see them and judge the best mummy."

Just before I'm helped into a standing position, I catch a brief glimpse of Kate coming towards me with more toilet paper. Suddenly, my vision vanishes as toilet paper is wrapped around my eyes. I feel strong hands lift me, and I'm turned to face in a different direction. My vision cut off, I start to panic and wriggle my body to escape the wrapping. My balance is lost, and I begin to tilt to one side.

I hear Mr. TDH's panicked voice call out, "Careful! She's falling!"

Suddenly the tilt is too much, and I feel my body fall. I grit my teeth as I wait to impact the ground. It's not the ground I hit, but instead, I splash into the pool. I hear screams as I hit the water, and I panic as I realize I might drown.

Fortunately, the makers of toilet paper have cleverly designed toilet paper to fall apart in water. I'm sure you understand why. My struggling arms and legs break free as the paper gets wet and soggy, and I clumsily attempt to swim to the pool edge. But before I reach it, I feel a hand grab me by my shirt collar and start to drag me to the edge. Other hands reach down and pull me out of the pool. I turn to thank my rescuer and realize it is Mr. TDH. He just smiles and says, "That's okay, Maddi. I was worried about you for a moment."

So then I spent the rest of the party soaked, but I still had a smile on my face because Mr. TDH had rescued me. Kaminko helped dry me off as best as she could and brushed my tangled hair into some sort of order.

Kate's response was, "Nice dive Maddi, but you wrecked all our good wrapping work."

I replied sarcastically, "Thanks for your concern. I'm fine."

Apart from that, it was a pleasant party, nice food, and I had a great time talking to Mr. TDH, Kamiko, and the other Japanese students. It would have been the perfect time to ask Mr. TDH about the card message, but we were never alone.

As we climbed into the car, Mom looked me up and down and asked, "Maddi did you go swimming in your clothes?"

Thanks for keeping an eye out for me, I thought, but replied, "No, Mom, I just sweated a lot."

Kamiko looked confused. I don't think she understands my sense of humor.

Wednesday

I arrived home from school to discover a flash Mercedes parked out the front and realized Kate's mother was visiting again. It was a happy visit because I heard them both laughing. I held my finger up to my lips to signal to Kamiko to be quiet and tried to lead her past the doorway to the lounge room, which was closed. Just as we drew level with the door, it opened, and Mom appeared in the doorway.

"I thought I heard you two arrive home, come in and say hello," she said.

Moms seem to have super-sensitive hearing when it comes to their children. She catches me every time.

So, we go in and say hi to Kate's mother and hear the news that we will be having another get-together on Saturday with a few friends and Kate's family. But this time, it will be at our house.

I've told Mom what Kate is like, but she insists I'm too judgemental and that I need to be more accepting of people.

Mom sees the good in everyone and expects I should aspire to be the same.

Thursday

While we are waiting for class, Gretel flirts happily with Tate. I subtly try to steer Mr. TDH away from the others so that we can have a discussion about the card. I have finally got him to myself when Kate comes running up, basically elbows me aside, and presents Mr. TDH with a wrapped present.

"What's this for?" he asks, seemly confused.

She replied, "It's just a small gift for helping me with my homework."

"That's not necessary," he replied, obviously embarrassed as he unwrapped the gift to reveal the latest FIFA play station game. He then continued, "I can't accept this. It's way too expensive."

"Don't be silly. It's nothing. Just enjoy it," Kate answered forcefully.

Just then, Tate wandered over, looking at the game still in Mr. TDH's hand. "Kate, where are you getting all this money from? That's the fifth expensive gift I've seen you give out to friends this week?" asked Tate.

Kate angrily snaps back, "Mind your own business, brother."

She storms off. The bell goes, which is a bit of a relief, as we are all standing there feeling a little awkward.

At lunchtime, Gretel and I discuss the strange conversation between the twins when Mr. TDH walks over. I asked, probably with a jealous tone in my voice, "When did you go over to Kate's house to help her with her homework?"

"I didn't," he replied defensibly. "I just emailed her the homework sheet when she messaged that she had lost hers."

Pretty generous gift for that, I thought, but I didn't say it out loud.

Unnoticed, Tate had arrived at our little group as we were talking, with a serious look on his face.

Gretel said, "What's with the argument between you and Kate about money? I thought you guys were rich?"

Tate sighed and explained, "Yes, my parents are quite wealthy, but they are very strict about only giving Kate and me a small weekly allowance. And to get that, we have to do a set list of chores. They both grew up in normal households and don't want their children growing up as spoilt rich kids."

Gretel smiled at Tate.

That was the perfect answer.

Chapter 9 - Five Finger Discount

Saturday

Mom had us up early to make sure everything was ready for our guests. Kamiko's introduction to an American mom's cleaning frenzy. She worked hard, and her only comment was, "Your Mom is very fussy."

After we had finished cleaning and organizing the garden furniture, Mom put us to work in the kitchen. Gretel had shown up by then, so all three of us helped make up the cake mix and some salad rolls. Both of which were new experiences for Kamiko, who especially enjoyed licking the spoon after we made the cake mix. The three of us got on so well. It was great fun.

The guests started arriving at about eleven am, and I was very happy to see Mr. TDH and his family arrive, along with his exchange student, Masa. I was not so happy when Linda Douglas arrived with Tate and Kate's family and their exchange student. Linda and Kate had become good friends at school, which shouldn't have surprised me, as in my eyes they were both as annoying as each other.

Once all the guests had arrived and settled in, Mom recruited all of the kids to serve up the food. Then the kids ate our food at the tables that were slightly removed from the parents.

The atmosphere at our tables was okay, although I felt a

little tense as Kate and Linda sat on either side of Mr. TDH. Grrrr!

Once again, Mom used us as waiters to clear the tables. Then Kate suggested we should ask if we could walk down to the mall, which was only a few minutes down the road. We all asked our respective parents, who readily agreed. Mr. TDH wasn't keen to go to a shopping mall with a group of girls, but Kate and Linda grabbed a hand each and dragged him along with us. Tate also seemed reluctant but walked along, chatting to Gretel. I wasn't happy with the hand-holding, but there was nothing I could do, so I just shrugged and followed along.

When we reached the mall, we split up into two groups. Mr. TDH led Tate and the Japanese students to the milkshake and ice cream parlor, while Kate led the rest of the girls into Macy's Department store, saying, "Let's check out the jewelry." Kate knew her way around the store, led us to the jewelry section straight away, and started picking up and admiring the necklaces on display. She asked Linda, "Do you think the exchange students would like these?"

After a while, she said, "Let's go and grab a milkshake, but just before we reached the exit door, she suddenly said, "Oh no, I must have left my phone behind, I'll just race back and get it, here Maddi can you take my bag with you, I don't want to lose it too." A strange thing to say, I thought but took it as she thrust it into my hands.

The rest of the girls and I headed to the doors, but as we left, the security alarm started to beep. We stopped, and suddenly a security guard appeared and called, "Maddi

76

Bull, what's going on? You're not robbing my store, are you?" I felt my face flush red but breathed a sigh of relief when I realized it was Dad's friend, Ted Stuart, the mall Security Guard. It's okay, girls. You can keep going. This old system malfunctions half the day lately.

We join the others at the ice cream parlor, closely followed by Kate. Kate asks for her bag back, then immediately starts rummaging around in it. She pulls out some necklaces, just like the ones she was looking at in the store, and then hands one to each of the Japanese students. I look at Gretel and Linda, and they look as shocked as I feel.

"Ah, Kate, can I talk to you outside for a moment?" I ask.

"Sure," she replies.

Outside I just asked her straight up if she had stolen the necklaces. She just smiled and said, "I refer to it as a five-finger discount. You see, I picked it up with my five fingers and placed it in my bag. Also, technically you stole it because you carried the bag containing the necklaces outside the store, not me. So, if you say anything, you'll get in trouble, not me."

I can't help it, my hands shoot up and cover my mouth as if by their own accord, and I start crying.

"Pull yourself together Maddi. You're only making yourself look guiltier." With that, she flounces back into the ice cream parlor, leaving me standing outside, still stunned.

I pull myself together as they all come out and start to walk back to my place. Gretel and Linda fall back to walk either side of me. "She stole those necklaces," Linda whispers.

"She must have," adds Gretel, "she didn't go anywhere near the cashier, and even if she did, you had her handbag."

"I don't know," I mumble and put my head down and walk faster. I can hear them still talking behind me, but I can't quite make out the words.

When we reach home, most people are getting ready to head off. As they all go, I say goodbye to Gretel and Mr. TDH, go to my bedroom and lay down. I don't know what to do about what Kate did, and I fall asleep with no solution found.

Sunday

I slept in until nine and woke still feeling stressed. As I sat having breakfast with Kamiko, Mom burst into the room with a cheerful, "Good morning girls, wasn't yesterday great? We really will have to do it again and soon."

I couldn't help it. I just burst into tears. Mom came and hugged me straight away and then took me to the lounge to talk to me. Tearfully I explained what had happened while Mom listened with a shocked look on her face.

"What will I do?" I asked Mom. "You don't have to do anything Maddi, your father and I will handle it." I breathed a big sigh of relief.

"But won't I get in trouble too?" I asked.

"No darling, you were involved unknowingly, so don't worry," replied Mom.

Monday

Both Kate and Tate were not at school today, and someone, probably Linda, had spread the story about Kate's stealing far and wide.

This created the rumors that they were both in jail, that they had fled the town and would never return to this school, and there was even a rumor that they had joined a crime gang in LA.

When I returned home, Mom told me the real story.

Mom and Dad had met with Kate's parents and told them what she had done on Saturday. They were shocked and angry and called both twins into the room in case Tate had any further knowledge of her activities. They asked my parents to stay there while they discussed what she had done. Mom said that initially, she had denied everything. However, when Tate mentioned other gifts she had been handing out before Saturday, she finally admitted to stealing the necklaces, as well as stealing several times earlier.

Mom said her parents would make Kate collect all the things she stolen and given way and return them to the shops she had taken them from. They also contacted the mall and arranged with the manager that she would be a volunteer unpaid cleaner for a month at the mall. Also, she would have to attend sessions with a counselor to try and ensure she would never re-offend.

Her parents were also grounding her for three months. Wow, I thought, crime doesn't pay. Mom also told me that both twins would still attend our school.

Tuesday

Kate and Tate's first day back was pretty hard on both of them. Some students teased her mercilessly with comments like quick hide your valuables.

At lunch, it was still happening, so I stood up and told the ones teasing, "Just back off, we all make mistakes, and Kate has been punished enough!"

That was enough to make them stop. Tate came over and thanked me.

Then Kate approached me, but instead of a thank you as I expected, she said with a snarl, "Don't think that makes up for telling on me. If it weren't for you, I wouldn't be in trouble."

I replied in a similar tone, "You have no one to blame but yourself. I didn't make you steal. That was your own decision."

I walked away and thought how proud Mom would have been if she could have seen me stand up for myself.

Chapter 10 - Editor Extraordinaire

Friday

It didn't take long for Kate to return to her normal self, dominating the class by always jumping in with answers first and volunteering for every class job offered. Let's face it, every kid wants a chance at a volunteer job at school, as it offers a chance to roam the school and escape the classroom for a while, kind of like a toilet break, only longer.

So today, when I returned from my toilet break tour, I walked into the classroom just in time to hear Granny, the principal, ask does anybody wish to volunteer. Desperate to get in ahead of Kate, I yell, "I'll do it!" I didn't even know what I had volunteered for.

Granny replies, "Thanks, it's good to finally get someone to volunteer. That's the third time I've had to ask. I'm sure you'll do a wonderful job, or at least an adequate job, as Editor of the Student Newsletter. What was your name again?"

Oops, that's not a job I wanted. I look around the class, Gretel has a look of sympathy on her face, as do most of the others, but Kate has a big smirk.

"Report to my office, Monday morning at eight o'clock, and I'll explain your duties and responsibilities."

Fantastic, now I get to start school before everyone else. It was a huge mistake! If I had known, I never would have volunteered for this.

Of course, Mom was over the moon when I told her of my new position as the newsletter editor. "Maddi, this could be the start of a fascinating career as a reporter," she gushed. "You could become famous like those Sixty Minute reporters."

"Do you mean like that Clark Kent guy?" I sarcastically asked.

Mom's not a fan of all those superhero series, so she didn't get that one at all.

Dad was nearly as excited. You would have thought I was going off to do Journalism at College.

Monday

I made sure I got to school early, as I didn't want to be late for the meeting with the principal. When I arrived there, the secretary told me to go straight in. I politely knocked on the half-opened door and entered the principal's lair. Oops, I meant office.

Her greeting to me was, "Are you in trouble again, Miss Bull?"

I suppose I should've been grateful that she remembered part of my name, but I wasn't impressed by her question. I reminded her about the meeting she wanted to have with me about the newsletter. That jogged her memory and earned me a ten-minute tirade about the enormous responsibility I would have on me as I was about to become the voice of the school.

It ended with a stern reminder that nothing goes in the newsletter without her permission and to see the secretary on the way out to be given computer access to the newsletter templates and access codes for publication to parents and students.

Friday

By now, I had realized just how much work was required to be the editor of the newsletter.

I had to get details of all school activities happening each fortnight and put them into a set template for the newsletter.

Plus, I was emailed a virtual flood of articles students wrote to be placed in the newsletter. Luckily Gretel and Mr. TDH had offered to help me out. It was SO much work, and I had to read each article and send the ones I thought would be okay for the newsletter to Granny to approve. Once that was done, I had to format them to fit into the newsletter proforma.

After a while, I realized Granny was much more content when she found some mistakes she could correct, so a couple of easy-to-spot deliberate mistakes sped up the whole process.

Each week Kate would send me some incredibly long and often boring article about something that few people would find of any interest at all. Articles about how Kate won her fifth gymnastics trophy, and her training system for cross country, were typical of the articles she submitted.

The end result was that my newsletter was a very dull thing to read.

Saturday

Today when the three of us were working on the newsletter to break the boredom, we decided to write a fictional article that wouldn't go in the newsletter. I suggested an article about how the school uses students as slaves to do what should be paid work around the school — even exposing how students were made to keep the gardens of the school staff in order. We also included how the school administrators had brought in Japanese students to bolster the workforce of the local student slaves.

We gathered together a few others and took pictures of a group of us pretending to work in the principal's yard.

At school, we took pictures of students with the cleaner's floor polisher and vacuums and some of the Japanese students in the school cafeteria kitchen.

In the end, we created a great report that looked very realistic, something Sixty Minutes would have been proud of. I, of course, made sure I kept a copy on my laptop as it carried my name, Maddi Bull - Editor and Investigative reporter. This would be a good memory of my editor's career. We only shared it with those involved and a few friends after swearing them not to talk about it or share it with anyone else.

Monday

On the way to school, I noticed quite many media cars driving around the local streets. Some cars had local TV station logos as well as some from neighboring towns and even a few from interstate.

Many kids were milling around at the school gate, and the gate was manned by the PE teacher, Mr. Sonic, and Granny the principal, stood beside him.

Outside the fence stood several people who looked like TV news reporters with crews setting up their cameras.

As I waited to enter the gate with Kamiko, I heard Granny, who had a megaphone in her hand, call out, "Attention all media people, you are not allowed to talk to any of the students without written parental permission, and that includes the Japanese students. Students, hurry up and get to your classes."

I heard one of the reporters call out to Granny, "Then you'll have to talk to us, at least give us a denial or a confirmation of the allegations."

Granny replied, "I'll be releasing a statement from the school later this morning. Until then, there will be no comment." Then she went back to urging the children to class.

As you can imagine, the whole school was obsessed with what on earth was going on, with our own media circus at the front gate. No one had a clue what it was about, including our teachers, but the first lessons in class were basically abandoned with students left to talk amongst themselves, as teachers had whispered discussion in the hallways.

Fantastic rumors were created. My favorite was that the Kardashian's children had enrolled in our school. Another was that alien transmissions had been detected coming from the school, and a time travel portal had opened in the school hall, and several students and teachers had disappeared into it. I thought that rumor was a little over the top!

Then the school intercom system announced that a special whole assembly was to be held in ten minutes in the hall. I guessed that knocked out the time travel portal rumor.

The teachers quickly moved us into the hall, and we saw Granny waiting out the front with an angry scowl on her face and the microphone in her hand.

No good morning students, she just blurted out, "Someone has put up on the internet a report claiming the students at our school, including our visiting Japanese students, are being used by the school as slave labor. Now the media are swarming our school to investigate these ridiculous claims. The report is very well written, so obviously, none of you have written it, but someone here must know who did it. I'm assuming an older sibling in university. So, if you have knowledge of this report, come to my office straight after the parade." She then turned, handed the microphone to a nearby teacher, and angrily strutted off.

I felt panic-stricken! I felt like the eyes of the whole school were focused on me. Of course, they weren't. It was just the few who helped me write the report and those we shared it with.

Gretel and Mr. TDH rushed over to me, "What are you going to do?" asked Gretel in a shaky voice.

"I'll have to own up to the report. It will come out eventually," I replied in an even shakier voice.

"We'll come with you," Gretel and Mr. TDH said in unison.

"No! There's no point in us all getting in trouble," I replied. But they insisted anyway, so the three of us trudged off to see Granny.

When we arrived at the office and told the secretary that we needed to talk to the principal, she merely asked, "About the report?"

"Yes," we told her. "Go straight in. The more the merrier," she said with a smirk.

I knock on the door, which is slightly closed, and enter, closely followed by Gretel and Mr. TDH. To my surprise, already in the room are Kate and Tate. I'm not sure what's going on.

Granny looks at us and says, "Maddi, are you involved in this too?" I take a deep breath and try to calmly explain why we wrote the article as a private joke and how it was never intended for publication.

Mr. TDH interrupted, saying, "All three of us were involved."

So I continued our explanation, saying that someone without our knowledge must have leaked the fictitious report to the media.

Granny points to Kate. "Yes, young Kate has already admitted to putting it up on Facebook and Instagram, and the media have picked it up from there. So, initially, I was looking at expulsion from our school for all involved for damaging our school's reputation. Then this wonderful young man, Tate, who brought his sister in to confess, has presented me with a wonderful solution that will not only save our school's good name but actually enhance it. This means that none of you will need be expelled. His idea, which I will obviously fine tune, is to announce to the media that the report was part of a school assignment to raise awareness of child workers being exploited in countries around the world. That the report was put up on social media to try and draw media attention so we can bring child worker exploitation into the spotlight. I will shortly hold a media conference where this will be revealed to the media. You three, as the writers of the article, will stand behind me at the conference, but you will not speak! You are only permitted to smile. If this works, you will not be given any punishment, but be aware, I will be keeping a very close eye on all of you from now on."

"Tate and Kate, you may now go back to class. You other three follow me," commanded Granny. She led us to the hall, where the media had finally been allowed into the school. About ten reporters and an array of cameras faced the front of the assembly area where Granny led us.

Granny read from her prepared speech, which was basically what she had already said to us, except more emphasis on her wonderful leadership to create such real-world interaction for her students and high academic standards.

Granny fielded a few questions where she continued to tell the media about the magnificent leadership at her school. One of the reporters asked if they could ask some questions about the students. Granny responded, "As much as I would love you to talk to our brilliant and articulate students, without written parental approval, it isn't allowed." She took a few more questions and then dismissed the gathered reporters like it was a school assembly. We were told to go back to class.

We were bombarded with questions when we returned to class but followed Granny's instructions by telling them to watch the news tonight to discover everything. As soon as school ended, I raced home and told Mom. She was excited to see me on TV but disappointed that I didn't get to speak.

Oh, and BTW, I did tell Mom the whole story. She was super impressed by the way our principal had turned it around. Dad, Mom, Kamiko, and I all sat waiting for the local news. They had cut out much of Granny's speech about herself. And in the end, the funniest thing happened. Mr. TDH made a peace sign behind my head. It was only on for a brief second, but I'm sure everyone would have seen it!

My parents burst into laughter. "Richard has a great sense of humor," said Dad. "And because your principal has lied, he will probably get away with it. Classic!"

Yep, that's my Richard, classic!

"Your boyfriend is hilarious," said Kamiko in a giggly voice.

Dad raised his eyebrows, "Boyfriend?" he asked.

I blushed as red as a tomato and replied, "We are just really good friends, Dad. I mean, I like him, but we aren't officially boyfriend/girlfriend."

"Well, Maddi," said Dad. "I think he's pretty cool, and if he was your boyfriend, I think I'd be okay with that, on certain conditions, and as long as you let us know and are honest with us."

At this moment, I wished the rumor about the aliens was true, and they would transport me into outer space. Instead, I murmured, "Thanks, Dad."

Chapter 11 – Sad Farewell

Wednesday

Sadly, the two week visit of Kamiko, and the other students, is coming to an end. Our last official function with the Japanese students was to be held at the school hall on Thursday with some special presentations, a dinner, and a dance. Then the students would spend one last night with their host families. All the host families felt the same sadness at the approaching departure of their Japanese students and tried to make the most of the last days together.

This afternoon, Mom took Kamiko and me, as well as Gretel and Mr. TDH and Masa, to the waterslide park as a final treat. The Japanese girls had never been to a waterpark, and they had a great time, although they were a little hesitant on the slides at first. Watching them swim made me look like an Olympic Games swimmer, as they could only do a little doggy style of paddling. The last thing we did was go down the longest and highest slide in the park. Masa and Kamiko insisted on going down last. We other three whizzed down with Gretel going the furthest at the end in the pool, then we gathered at the edge to await the other two girls.

Masa came next and landed with a yell and a huge splash. We heard Kamiko screaming all the way down, finally emerging at speed and being driven to the bottom of the pool. The screaming must have drawn the attention of the lifeguard, and when Kamiko hadn't emerged from the bottom of the pool, the lifeguard ripped off her hat and dived into the pool, quickly dragging Kamiko to the edge. In the excitement, Kaminko forgot her English and was blurting out something in Japanese. The lifesaver and all of us were confused until Masa translated what Kamiko had said, "That was so much fun much! That was the best!"

That night Kamiko presented us with some special presents as a thank you for hosting her. She gave Mom a beautiful paper fan and Dad a calligraphy pen. But I was given the most beautiful gift of all, a beautiful red kimono dress. Naturally, I tried it on straight away, and in all modesty, I looked amazing.

Thursday

It was a fairly relaxed day at school, with most of our time spent organizing and rehearsing for the official farewell tonight. The Japanese girls taught their host students a traditional Japanese dance to perform at the farewell. It was a little tricky, but we eventually mastered it. It would look extra good because all the female student hosts had also been given kimonos in a different color for each person.

When we returned home, I helped Kamiko pack her suitcase, and then we took the dogs for a walk one last time. Soon it was time to get ready. Kamiko helped me put on the kimono and put my hair up for me. Kamiko wore a blue kimono. Once we were both dressed, Mom set up the camera on the timer and got a picture of the whole family. Then we headed off to school.

The hall looked great, with so many students wandering around with their colorful outfits. The speeches from the principal were a bit long, the food was good, but the dancing was the fun part. When we did the Japanese dance, the parents and other students loved it. Then our visitors did another traditional Japanese dance which was a bit more intricate than ours. It was amazing!

Once the formal parts were over, they started playing more modern music, and all the students started doing disco dancing. It was great fun, with groups of us dancing together, trying to outdo each other with the best moves.

Eventually, I got really hot, so I moved outside to cool off and discovered Mr. TDH outside, obviously with the same idea. We talked about how much we would miss our exchange students and how much fun tonight had been. He even complimented me on how good I looked in the kimono. This was it, I thought, finally, the chance to ask what was written on the message from him that Buddy had destroyed. "Richard," I began, "remember how you gave me that card before you went on holiday with your parents? Well, Buddy chewed it up that same night, and part of it was destroyed so that I couldn't read it."

He replied, "Buddy is such a cutie, isn't he, but a bit of a devil at times. Remember that time he peed on my new shirt?" Yep Buddy is cute, I thought, but I don't want to talk about him right now. So I said, "Yes, he is the best, but I need to know what you wrote on the last part of the card. What was it you were going to ask me?"

"Oh, that was a long time ago. It doesn't really matter," he responded.

I wasn't going to let it go that easily! I've been waiting for months to find out what he wanted to ask me. "No, Richard, I've wondered about this for months. I have to know. You've got to tell me!" I demanded.

"Okay, sorry, it was no big deal. I just asked if you would return my library books. I left them in my desk," he replied in a voice slightly confused by my insistence.

How embarrassed I felt, I'm sure you can imagine. Here I was thinking he was going to ask me to be his girlfriend, and he just wanted his library books returned.

"Okay, thanks, I've got to go," I replied and bolted back to the hall with my red glowing face lighting the way. I grabbed Gretel and dragged her to a vacant corner, and told her about my conversation. She hugged me and took me back to dance with our Japanese friends.

Friday

We all woke a little later in the morning and ate breakfast quickly. Mom gave Kamiko a copy of the photo she took of us, in a lovely frame.

Kamiko had tears in her eyes as she thanked Mom and Dad for the photos and for hosting her. Mom teared up a little as well. She is such a loving person.

Today, Kamiko wanted to walk to school. I think because she wanted to extend our time together. It was a lovely day, and we talked about how much we had enjoyed each other's company.

Once inside the gate, it was time to part. Kamiko gave me a hug and said, "One day, you must visit me in Japan. Hopefully, your school will do a return exchange."

By now, we were both crying, and I could hardly get out the words. "I hope so."

She walked to the hall to meet up with the other exchange students who were waiting for the bus to take them to the airport.

I walked to my classroom to gather with the other host students who were either crying like me or at least had very red-looking eyes.

Soon the teacher came in and asked us to go to our seats and to take out our books.

So life was going back to normal, or so I thought.

Thank you for reading this book!

I would really appreciate it if you could leave a review.
Thank you!!!

Bill - *An Almost Cool Dad*

BE SURE TO CHECK OUT
OUR BEST SELLING
COLORING BOOKS, JOURNALS & DIARIES.

KIDS ALL OVER THE WORLD
LOVE THESE BOOKS!

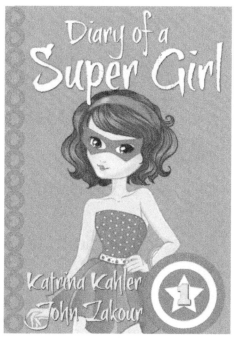

THANK YOU

We really appreciate and love
our readers! You are amazing!
If you loved this book, we would really
appreciate it if you could leave a review
on Amazon.

You can subscribe to our website
www.bestsellingbooksforkids.com
so we can notify you as soon as
we release a new book.

Please Katrina's Facebook page
https://www.facebook.com/katrinaauthor
and follow Katrina on Instagram
@katrinakahler

Printed in Great Britain
by Amazon

20155135R10068